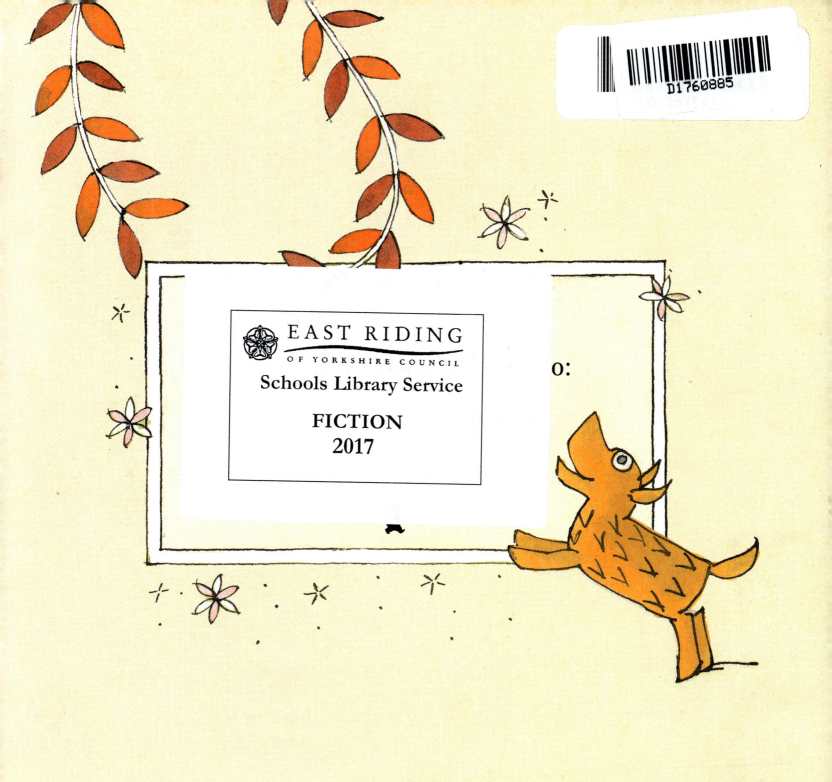

To Astrid and Helena

DAVID LUCAS

GRENDEL

A CAUTIONARY TALE ABOUT
CHOCOLATE

First published 2013 by Walker Books Ltd, 87 Vauxhall Walk, London SE11 5HJ   This edition published 2014   4 6 8 10 9 7 5 3
© 2013 David Lucas   The right of David Lucas to be identified as author/illustrator of this work has been asserted by him in
accordance with the Copyright, Designs and Patents Act 1988   This book has been typeset in New Century Schoolbook
Printed in China   All rights reserved. No part of this book may be reproduced, transmitted or stored in an information retrieval
system in any form or by any means, graphic, electronic or mechanical, including photocopying, taping and recording, without prior
written permission from the publisher.   British Library Cataloguing in Publication Data: a catalogue record for this book is
available from the British Library   ISBN 978-1-4063-5254-2   www.walker.co.uk

WALKER BOOKS
AND SUBSIDIARIES

LONDON · BOSTON · SYDNEY · AUCKLAND

Grendel loved his mum.
Grendel loved his dog.

But most of all Grendel LOVED
chocolate.

"I bought you a chocolate egg,"
said Grendel's mum.
"CHOCOLATE!"
said Grendel.
"Give it to me!
Give it to me!"

"I was only going to
give it to you if
you were good,"
said Mum.

"I'll be good.
I'll be good..."

Grendel snatched
the chocolate egg
and ran.

He sat in his secret hiding place.

Mmm … *delicious.*

Inside the chocolate egg was a note.
A note?
You have three wishes, it said.

"Three wishes?" said Grendel
He didn't believe in magic.

"I just wish I had MORE
chocolate!" he said.

He was just about to wish the WHOLE WORLD
was chocolate when he stopped...
No. He had to be SENSIBLE.

"I know!" he said.
"I wish ... everything
I *touch* turns
to chocolate!"

The note was chocolate.
YUM!
He was sitting on a chocolate log.
SNAP!
MMM.

He turned the trees
to chocolate.
DELICIOUS!

And the path.
SLURP!

And the rocks.
CRUNCH!

It was so much fun …

until the dog
came to meet him.

"NO!" said Grendel.

"Grendel!
What have you done?"
said Mum.

"NOOOO!!" said Grendel.
"Mum! Mum! Speak to me, Mum!"
But she didn't say a word.

"I *hate* chocolate!"

he roared.

"I hate it!
I hate it!
I HATE it!"

The sun was hot.
Mum ... was ...
starting ... to ...
melt!

"What have I done?" said Grendel.
He was just about to say that
he wished he wasn't so stupid
– when he stopped…

"I've got *one more* wish!
Think, Grendel, think. *Carefully*."

He had an idea. He closed his eyes
and crossed his claws.
"I wish …

"it was ... YESTERDAY!"

His pillow wasn't chocolate.
Or his blanket.

He heard singing.

What a wonderful, familiar sound!

"Mum!" he cried.
"You're not chocolate!"
"Me? Chocolate?"
she laughed.
"No, dear."

He hugged her for a
long, long time. And then
he hugged the dog.

"What's happened to you?"
she said.
"You're so different!"
Then she smiled.
"You are a good little
monster really."

"Look, I bought you a
chocolate egg!"
"You have it," said Grendel.
"*Grendel?* Are you sure?"
"Yes, Mum. But if
there's a little
note inside…"

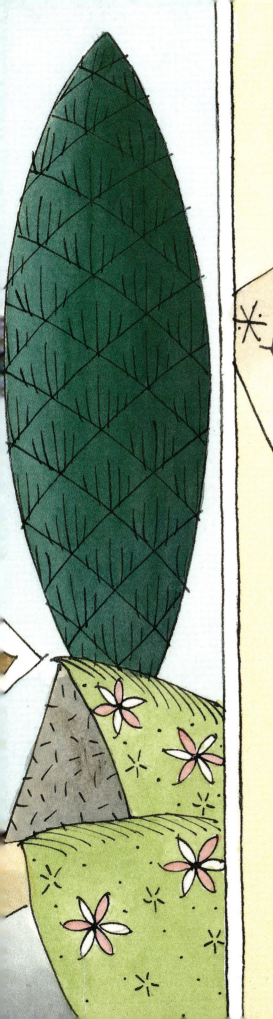

There WAS a little note inside.
"YOU HAVE THREE WISHES."

And he told her the whole story.
And of course the moral of this story
is to be careful what you wish for.

And they were …

VERY careful indeed!

Internationally acclaimed author/illustrator **David Lucas**
has been writing stories and inventing imaginary worlds since
he was a teenager. Born in Middlesbrough, in his childhood
he moved to London, where he now lives and works.
"I believe the world is alive with magic," he says,
"and it's that feeling that really inspires my work."

Other books by David Lucas:

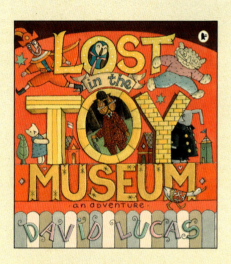 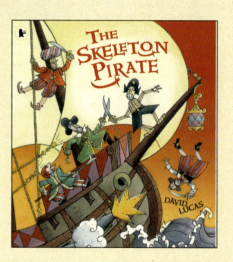

Available from all good booksellers

www.walker.co.uk